Iggy Pig's
Skippy Day

Written by   Illustrated by

Vivian
French

David
Melling

Hodder
Children's
Books

A division of Hodder Headline Limited

For David M.
with many thanks
Love Viv

For Daniel Hall
D. M.

Iggy Pig was skipping.

"Watch me skip, Mother Pig!
Watch me skip!"

"OINK!" said Mother Pig. "I'm watching, my own dear little pig. Now don't go skipping too far!"

Iggy Pig went skipping around
the farmyard.

"Skip skip skip
I can skip all day
Over the hills and far away!"
he sang.

On top of the
haystack was a
big grey animal.

The big grey animal
woke and listened.
"AHA!" said the big
grey animal. "AHA!"

The big
grey animal slid
off the haystack.
"Cooee, Iggy Pig.
Cooee!"

4

Iggy Pig never stopped skipping.
"Who are you?" he asked.

"Just a friend," said the big grey
animal. "Iggy Pig, Iggy Pig –
may I skip with you?"

"Yes, yes!" said Iggy Pig.

"Do come and skip with me!"

Iggy Pig went skipping through
the gate.

The big grey
animal skipped
behind him.

"Skip skip skip

We can skip all day

Over the hills and far away!"

sang Iggy Pig.

"Cluck! Cluck! Iggy Pig!"
clucked Chicky Chick.
"May I skip with you?"

"Yes, yes, Chicky Chick!"
said Iggy Pig.
"Do come and
skip with us!"

Iggy Pig went skipping down
the lane.

The big grey animal skipped
behind him.

Chicky Chick skipped behind
the big grey animal.

"Skip skip skip

We can skip all day

Over the hills and far away!"

sang Iggy Pig.

"Baa! Baa! Iggy Pig!"

called Lucky Lamb.

"May I skip with you?"

"Yes, yes, Lucky Lamb!" said Iggy

Pig. "Do come and skip with us!"

Iggy Pig went skipping across
the field.

The big grey animal skipped
behind him.

Chicky Chick skipped behind
the big grey animal.

Lucky Lamb skipped behind
Chicky Chick.

"Skip skip skip

We can skip all day

Over the hills and far away!"

sang Iggy Pig.

Bunny Rabbit was under the trees.
She saw Iggy Pig skipping across
the field.

"Iggy Pig! Iggy Pig!
Where are you going?"
"Hello, Bunny Rabbit!" said Iggy
Pig. "Come and skip with us."

Iggy Pig went skipping up
the hill.

The big grey animal skipped
behind him.

Chicky Chick skipped behind
the big grey animal.

Lucky Lamb skipped behind
Chicky Chick.

Bunny Rabbit skipped behind
Lucky Lamb.

"Skip skip skip

We can skip all day

Over the hills and far away!"

sang Iggy Pig.

At the top of the hill Iggy Pig
skipped in a circle. The big grey
animal skipped behind him.

"Cluck! Cluck!" clucked
Chicky Chick.
"Iggy Pig, I have skipped too
far! I want to go home to
my farmyard!"

"Baa! Baa!" said Lucky Lamb.

"I want to go home to my field!"

"That's right!" said Bunny
Rabbit. "It's time to go home,
Iggy Pig!"

Iggy Pig did not stop skipping.

"No no!" he said, "I can skip all day. Over the hills and far away!"

"That's right, Iggy Pig," said the big grey animal. "And I will skip with you wherever you go!"

Iggy Pig went skipping over
the hill.
The big grey animal skipped
behind him.

"Skip skip skip
We can skip all day
Over the hills and far away!"
sang Iggy Pig.

Bunny Rabbit, Lucky Lamb and
Chicky Chick went home.

Dusty Dog was running around
the farmyard.

"Where have you been, Chicky
Chick?" he asked.

"I've been skipping," said Chicky
Chick. "I've been skippng with
Iggy Pig."

"And where is Iggy Pig now?"
asked Dusty Dog.
"Over the hills and far away,"
said Chicky Chick.

"I see," said Dusty Dog.
"And is he on his own?"
"Oh NO," said Chicky Chick.
"There's a big grey animal
skipping just behind him."

"WOOF!" said Dusty Dog.

"WOOF! WOOF! WOOF!"

Dusty Dog dashed out of
the farmyard.

"Cluck! Cluck!" clucked Chicky Chick. "Dusty Dog has gone to skip with Iggy Pig!"

Iggy Pig was still skipping.
The big grey animal skipped
behind him.

"Iggy Pig, Iggy Pig," said the big
grey animal. "Shall we stop for
a rest?"

"No, no!" said Iggy Pig,

and he skipped faster.

The big grey animal began to puff.

Iggy Pig went skipping down
the hill.
The big grey animal puffed
behind him.

"Iggy Pig, Iggy Pig,"
puffed the big grey animal.
"I think we should stop for
a rest. I think we should stop
for a drink."

"No, NO!" said Iggy Pig,

and he skipped faster than ever.

The big grey animal began

to pant.

Iggy Pig went skipping around
the hill.
The big grey animal puffed and
panted behind him.

"Iggy Pig! Iggy Pig! It's time
to stop! Iggy Pig! Iggy Pig!
I'm hungry!"

"No, no!" said Iggy Pig, and he
skipped higher and higher.

The big grey animal began
to limp.

Iggy Pig skipped back across
the field.

The big grey animal puffed and
panted and limped behind him.

"Stop, Iggy Pig! Stop!"
he panted.

"No, no!" said Iggy Pig as he
skipped round and round.

"Iggy Pig!" growled
the big grey animal. "If you don't
stop skipping AT ONCE I shall
eat you ALL UP!"

"Oh no," said Iggy Pig. "You'll have to catch me first." And Iggy Pig went skipping down the lane.

The big grey animal stopped. "I just can't skip another step," he moaned.

The big grey animal sat down
JUST as Dusty Dog dashed up.
"OH! OH! OH!" moaned the big
grey animal.

"WOOF!" barked Dusty Dog, and
he chased the big grey animal.
"WOOF! WOOF! WOOF!"

He chased him across the field
and over the hill.

He chased him over the hills and
far away.

Iggy Pig skipped all the way
home to the farmyard.
"Skip skip skip
I skipped all day
Over the hills and far away!"
sang Iggy Pig.

"Did you skip ALL day, my dear
Iggy Pig?" asked Mother Pig.

"Yes," said Iggy Pig.

"Bunny Rabbit, Lucky Lamb and Chicky Chick couldn't skip like me. Even the big grey animal couldn't skip like me."

"OINK!" said Mother Pig.

"OINK! OINK! OINK! Iggy Pig! Iggy Pig! Have you been skipping with a WOLF?"

Iggy Pig didn't answer.

Iggy Pig was fast asleep.